Wha

Written by Jo Windsor

Rigby

Look at this seal.
It can make
its nose big.

It can make
a loud noise
with its big nose.

This animal has
a big nose, too.

It likes to swim
under the water.
It can shut its nose
when it goes
under the water.

This animal has
a very big nose.

It lives in a place
where the air
is very cold.
Its big nose helps
to make the air warm.

This animal
has a long nose.

Its long nose helps it
find food.
It likes to eat
mice and insects.

This animal has a nose
that looks like
a long worm.

It can find food
with its long nose.
It likes to eat ants.

Look at this nose!

This animal lives
under the ground.
Its nose helps it
find its food.

Index

Guide Notes

Title: What a Nose!
Stage: Early (3) – Blue

Genre: Nonfiction (Expository)
Approach: Guided Reading
Processes: Thinking Critically, Exploring Language, Processing Information
Written and Visual Focus: Photographs (static images), Labels, Index

Thinking Critically

(sample questions)

- Tell the children this book is about animals with different noses.
- Look at the title and read it to the children.
- Ask the children what they know about animals with different noses.
- Focus the children's attention on the Index. Ask: "What are you going to find out about in this book?"
- If you want to find out about long noses, on which pages would you look?
- If you want to find out about big noses, on which pages would you look?
- Look at the animals on pages 2 and 10. What is different about their noses?
- Why do you think the animal on page 4 shuts its nose when it goes under the water?
- What else do you think an animal might use its nose for?

Exploring Language

Terminology

Title, cover, photographs, author, photographers

Vocabulary

Interest words: seal, nose, water, air, warm, long, food, worm
High-frequency words: has, help, too

Print Conventions

Capital letter for sentence beginnings, periods, commas, exclamation mark

Titles in the series

The Air Stewardess 0–241–11209–5
The Dustman 0–241–11210–9
The Doctor 0–241–11415–2
The Farmer 0–241–10937–X
The Fireman 0–241–10936–1
The Fisherman 0–241–11414–4
The Hairdresser 0–241–11211–7
The Lorry Driver 0–241–11164–1
The Milkman 0–241–10934–5
The Nurse 0–241–11162–5
The Policewoman 0–241–10935–3
The Postman 0–241–11163–3
The Shop-keeper 0–241–11416–0
The Soldier 0–241–11417–9
The Vet 0–241–11165–X
The Zoo-keeper 0–241–11212–5

The author and publishers would like to thank the following people for their hospitality and co-operation during the production of this book: Corporal Nigel Isaac, Mr D. Knight of the Ministry of Defence, Lt. Col. R.E. Wills RCT and Captain A.S. Taylor RCT, and everyone else at Buller Barracks. They would also like to thank the RCT for permission to reproduce the photographs on page 3.

Layout by Andrew Shoolbred

First published in Great Britain 1985 by
Hamish Hamilton Children's Books
Garden House, 57–59 Long Acre, London WC2E 9JZ

British Library Cataloguing in Publication Data
Stewart, Anne
The soldier.—(Cherrystones)
1. Great Britain. *Army*—Military life—Juvenile literature
I. Title II. Fairclough, Chris III. Series
355.1′0941 U767

ISBN 0–241–11417–9

Typeset by Katerprint Co Ltd, Oxford

Printed in Great Britain by
Cambus Litho Ltd East Kilbride Scotland

CHERRYSTONES

The Soldier

Anne Stewart

Photographs by
Chris Fairclough

Hamish Hamilton · London

'Has this boot been polished?'
'Yes sir. I did it last night.'

It is 7 a.m. and Corporal Nigel Isaac of the Royal Corps of Transport (RCT) is inspecting recruits from Intake 155 – their uniforms, lockers and sleeping quarters. Nigel is in charge of sixty recruits, who have come to Aldershot in Hampshire for ten weeks' basic training. After this, they will be sent to Yorkshire for driver training, and then posted to their first working squadron. This could be in Britain, or overseas – in Germany, Cyprus or Belize.

The RCT's job is to organise, man, and operate all transport needed by the Army in peace and war. When necessary, it also helps the Royal Air Force and the Royal Navy. Here you can see a few of the vehicles under its command.

Motorcycles are ridden by Corporals. In this picture, one motorcycle leads a convoy of trucks. Trucks are used to carry a variety of loads – for example, soldiers, food and ammunition.

This load-bearer is specially designed to travel over rough, swampy ground.

Lessons start at 8 o'clock. Today's first lesson is marching (drill). The recruits go to the armoury to collect their rifles and magazines. (This type of magazine is a container for bullets.) Nigel's recruits are in their ninth week of training, and have been doing drill with rifles for four weeks.

When the recruits are on the parade ground, they quickly attach straps (or slings) to their rifles. All the slings have to be on the inside of the magazine. Then they wait for the order to 'fall in'.

'Left, right, left, right . . .'
New recruits are taught to shout the commands together. It helps them to march in time, and to learn the different steps more quickly. By the ninth week, only one recruit voices the commands. Nigel's recruits can now march, change step, turn and present arms without difficulty.

Nigel inspects the recruits. He checks they have all washed and shaved properly, and that their hair is cut short. Their uniforms must be clean and pressed, and their boots polished. Nigel inspects one rank at a time. The men in this rank stand stiffly to attention; those in the other two stand 'at ease'.

After drill, the recruits change into 'combat dress'. This is the uniform they would wear in battle. They hurry to the shooting range for rifle practice. Before the lesson begins, they put specially-fitted ear-plugs into their ears to protect them from the noise of the guns. Nigel wears ear mufflers.

The recruits learn to shoot in three positions – standing, kneeling, and lying down. They each fire at one target 30 metres away. They aim at the middle of their target. The bullet holes should be as close together as possible.

'Try to control your breathing,' Nigel advises.

'If you always pull the trigger just before you breathe in, you will have a better chance of hitting the same spot each time.'

Each group of six recruits fires five bullets. When the last person has fired, everyone walks forward to inspect the targets.

'You didn't keep your breathing steady, did you?' says Nigel.

'Look where this bullet is!'

Nigel talks to each recruit in turn. He compliments them on the good shots and explains what has gone wrong on the bad ones. Then the recruits paste little paper squares over the holes, so that the next group of recruits will be able to identify their shots.

Before lunch, Nigel changes back into his lightweight trousers and sweater. This is his everyday uniform. He has two white stripes on his right sleeve to show he is a Corporal.

He sees Lance-Corporal Porter outside the guard room. She is waiting to drive a visiting General to the Officers' Mess for lunch. There are over 400 women soldiers in Aldershot who perform a variety of duties. They drive staff cars for senior officers, or work as clerks, cooks or signallers. Unlike armies in some other countries, women soldiers in Britain are not trained to fight. But they are taught to defend themselves.

Lunch for Nigel is in the Dining Hall. Everyone eats here except the Sergeants and Commissioned Officers. They each have their own Mess.

The soldiers have a choice of several main courses, and they can take as much as they want. Most of the new recruits eat a lot after their morning's exercise. Fitter soldiers like Nigel are usually less hungry.

All the Corporals eat together in a separate section of the Dining Hall.

To become soldiers, all recruits must be fit, strong and ready for action. Most of the physical training takes place on the 'assault course'. Here Nigel shows them how to scramble over high walls, jump across ditches, run up steep slopes, and climb ropes.

To make them work harder, he sometimes divides them into two teams and races them round the course.

'Come on, Robinson,' he shouts. 'You can go faster than that!'

When a new Intake of recruits first arrives, Nigel often has to teach them how to keep themselves clean and tidy. Some have never washed or ironed their own clothes before. One job all recruits soon become skilled at is polishing (or 'bulling') their boots. It takes a lot of work to make them shine as brightly as these.

A week or two later, Nigel can start to teach them more difficult skills. Here he is demonstrating how to take apart a Light Machine Gun (LMG). It is important that every soldier knows how to do this in order to keep his gun in good working order.

During their ten weeks' training, all recruits spend four days 'on exercise'. This is when they begin to learn how to survive in battle. The exercise normally takes place in woods a few kilometres from the barracks.

One of the first things the recruits learn to do is dig a trench. Each trench must be shoulder-deep and wide enough to hold at least two men. It takes about four hours to dig. After it has been disguised with branches and leaves, soldiers inside it could shoot at an enemy without being seen.

The recruits also have to learn how to camouflage themselves. This is called 'scrimming up'. They cover themselves with ferns and twigs and, if necessary, spread special dark-coloured cream over their faces. They blend into the background.

For each day's meals, every recruit is given a 24-hour ration pack (or 'compo'). This usually contains one tin of meat for each meal (sausage perhaps, or steak and kidney pie), packets of dried vegetables, powdered coffee and drinking chocolate, plus a few bars of chocolate.

Towards dusk, the recruits look for a comfortable piece of flat ground to sleep on. They clear away any twigs or stones that might dig into them during the night, and spread out their sleeping bags. Everyone lies fairly close together for safety.

The ideal place to sleep is between two trees. The recruit can then tie each end of a plastic sheet (a 'poncho') to one of the trees, and so make a kind of tent. This tent, or 'basha', will protect him from the rain and dew. The recruits go to bed fully dressed, with their gun beside them. They must be ready in case of enemy attack.

On the last day of training, the successful recruits take part in a 'Passing-out parade'. At its end, they will no longer be recruits, but fully trained soldiers. Parents and friends watch proudly as Nigel leads them on to the parade ground. All the soldiers are wearing 'Number 2 Dress', the smartest and most formal of their uniforms. It is only worn on parades and other special occasions.

The recruits march around the parade ground and halt in the centre. Facing the Inspecting Officer, they stand to attention and present arms. The Inspecting Officer then goes forward to inspect the troops and congratulate them. He spends a few moments chatting to each soldier.

Meanwhile, Nigel's next Intake of recruits watches from the barracks windows.

'Will we ever look as good as that?' they wonder.

After the parade is over and the new soldiers have left, Nigel runs the 12 kilometres back home. He runs to and from work every day.

Nigel and his wife, Elaine, bought their house when they came back from Germany. Elaine was a driver then, serving in the same squadron as Nigel. Now she works at Heathrow Airport.

Soon Nigel will be posted somewhere else – and though he and Elaine both like being in Aldershot, they are looking forward to being on the move again. Soldiers are given a new posting every two to three years.

'I could never work in an office,' says Nigel. 'That's why I joined the Army. What other job offers the chance to travel all over the world?'

Index